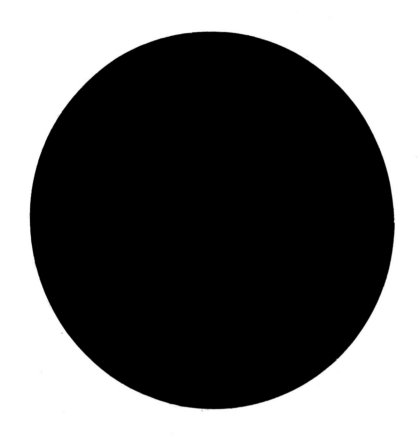

the holes are cut at Schildts!

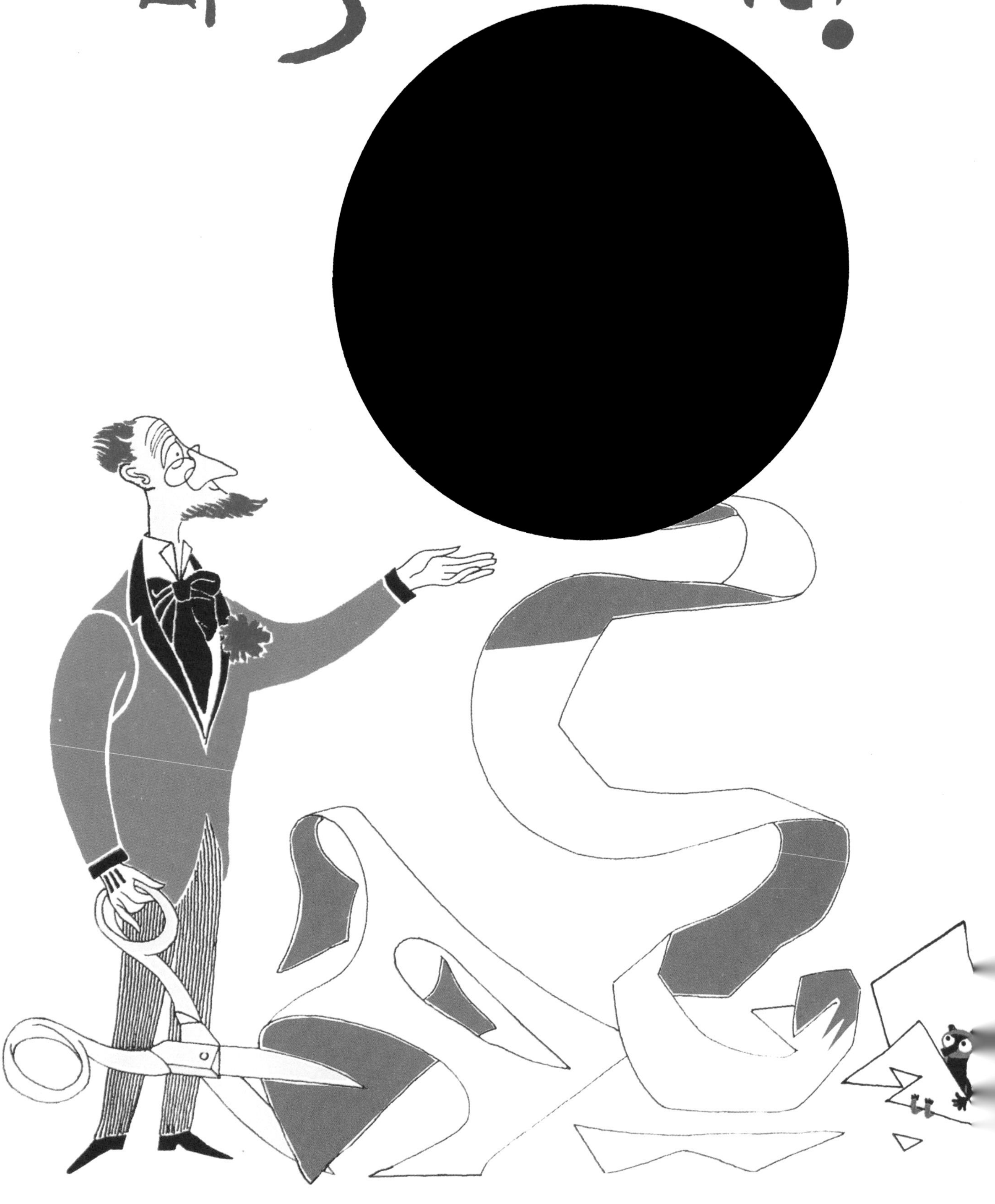

TOVE JANSSON

MOOMIN, MYMBLE
AND LITTLE MY

ENGLISH VERSION BY SOPHIE HANNAH

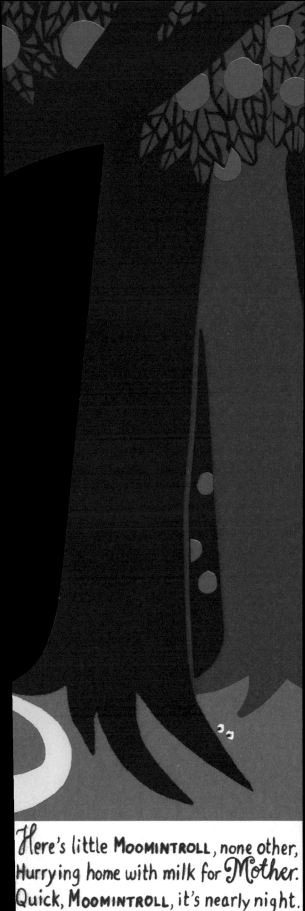

Here's little **MOOMINTROLL**, none other,
Hurrying home with milk for **Mother**.
Quick, **MOOMINTROLL**, it's nearly night.
Run home while there's a bit of light.

Don't hang around in **WOODS** like these.
Strange creatures lurk between the trees.
The wind begins to howl and hiss.
NOW, GUESS WHAT HAPPENS AFTER *THIS*.

Beyond the forest, bathed in light,
The air tastes fresh. The grass glows bright.
The sun shines down on fields of flowers.
MOOMINTROLL's walked for hours and hours
But, happy to be homeward bound,
He kicks his legs and leaps around.
He sees a TALL shape. A house? His own?
How very TALL the chimney's grown
When yesterday the roof was FLAT.
WELL, GUESS WHAT HAPPENED AFTER THAT.

'That's not a roof or chimney pot
It's *Mymble*'s hair, tied in a knot
She's weeping on a big tin can,
Poor thing,' thought MOOMINTROLL, and ra
To *Mymble*, begging, 'Please don't cry
'I've lost my sister, LITTLE MY,'
She told him, and began to yelp.
'She ran away! Oh, MOOMIN, help!'
MOOMINTROLL frowned. 'Well, let's begin
By checking if she's in this tin.
Some villain might have stashed her in it.
NOW GUESS WHAT HAPPENS IN A **MINUTE**

Portrait
of the lost
little
MY.

They crawl out on the other side
Next to a river, deep and wide,
Where GAFFSIE, with her gruesome hair,
Gives them a mean and chilling stare
And growls, 'YOU FOOLS! I'LL MAKE YOU WISH
YOU'D STAYED AT HOME. NOW LET ME FISH.'

Mymble says, 'Quick, let's go. She'll bite.'
And MOOMINTROLL says, 'Yes, quite right.
Perhaps your sister's in this cave?'
They tiptoe in. They must be brave,
And find poor LITTLE MY somehow.
WELL, GUESS WHAT HAPPENS TO THEM NOW.

Among the boulders piled up high
There is no sign of LITTLE MY.
They search and search but find no trace.
The bitter wind whips *Mymble*'s face.
MOOMINTROLL feels extremely glum.
He wants HIS *HOME*, HIS *BED*, HIS *MUM*.
Where is the warm and sunny day?
THEN GUESS WHAT HAPPENED **RIGHT AWAY**.

HEMULEN, with a vacuum hose
Had got some house dust up his nose.
Spring cleaning (though it wasn't Spring)
Was HEMULEN's most favourite thing.
DISASTER *STRUCK*.
                His greedy hoover,
Sucking hard enough to move a

MOUNTAIN, SWALLOWED BOTH OUR FRIENDS
INTO ITS TUBE. AROUND THE BENDS
BOTH MOOMINTROLL AND *Mymble* FLEW.
MOOMINTROLL'S MILK WAS SUCKED UP TOO.

He shouted, through the
                    gunge and fluff,

'OH, *Mother*, HELP, I'VE HAD **ENOUGH!'**

A stroke of luck! Who should walk by
But *Mymble*'s sister, LITTLE MY.
While taking a relaxing stroll
She'd heard the cries of MOOMINTROLL.
She cut the tube and pulled it back.
Mymble and MOOMINTROLL were black
With dust from head to toe. MY laughed.
'BLIMEY, THE TWO OF YOU LOOK DAFT!'
'We've saved you, MY!' cheered *Mymble*, 'Phew!'
HEMULEN, see thing through and through,
Chased them away like DUST and MESS -
AND GUESS WHAT HAPPENED. GO ON, *GUESS.*

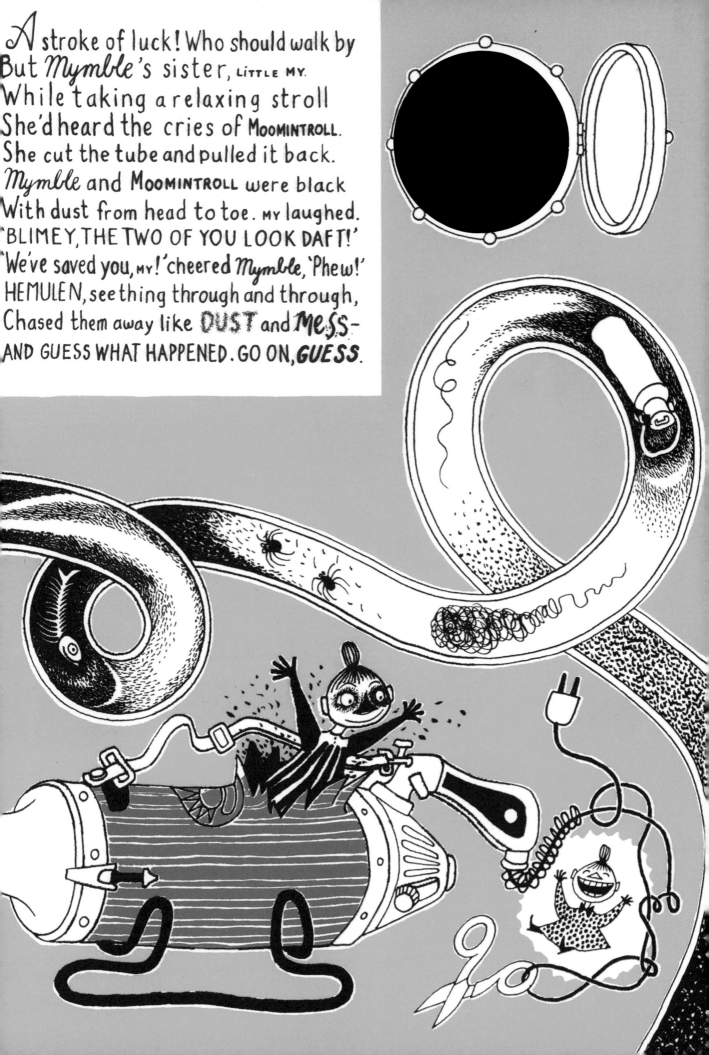

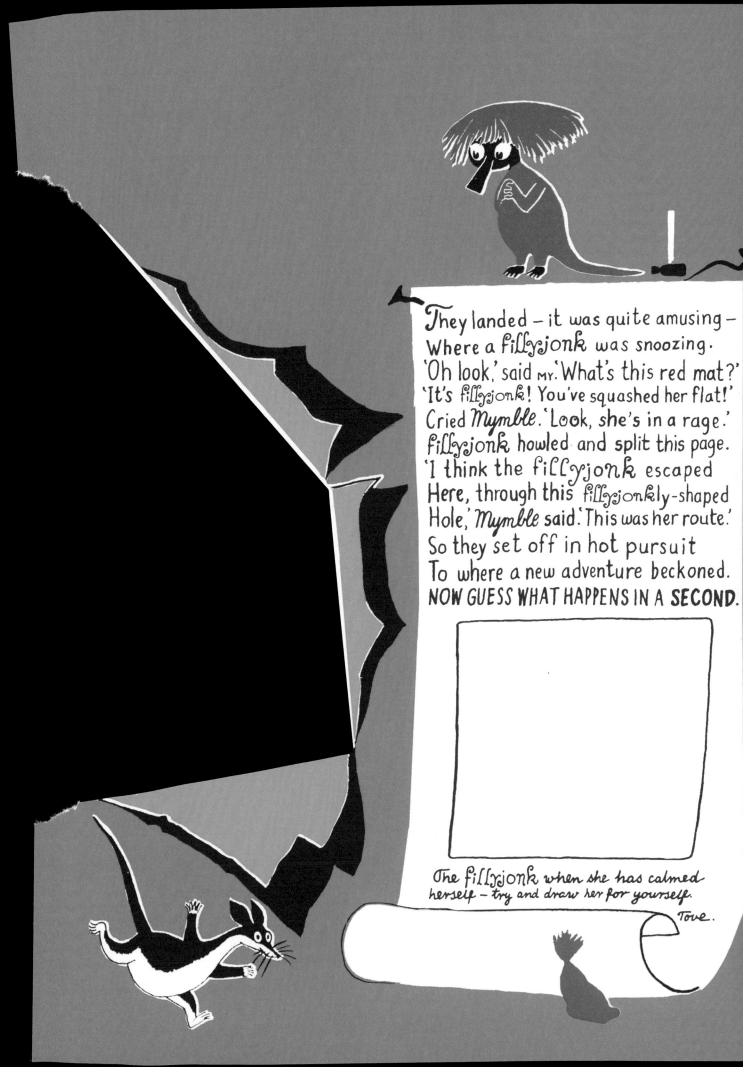

They landed – it was quite amusing –
Where a fillyjonk was snoozing.
'Oh look,' said Mr.'What's this red mat?'
'It's fillyjonk! You've squashed her flat!'
Cried Mymble.'Look, she's in a rage.'
fillyjonk howled and split this page.
'I think the fillyjonk escaped
Here, through this fillyjonkly-shaped
Hole,' Mymble said.'This was her route.'
So they set off in hot pursuit
To where a new adventure beckoned.
NOW GUESS WHAT HAPPENS IN A SECOND.

The fillyjonk when she has calmed
herself – try and draw her for yourself.

Tove.

The hunt is not a huge success.
They find the fillyjonk's red dress
But as for fillyjonk the creature,
Sad to say, she doesn't feature.
'Golly, now she'll have to buy
A brand new dress,' says LITTLE MY.
A storm flares up. The lightning flashes.
On the beach, a wild Wave crashes.
It simply shouldn't be so scary,
Bringing milk back from the dairy.
'My Mother needs this milk tonight,'
Says MOOMINTROLL. 'Oh, look, a light!'
A sign of life, a friend, a guide?
NOW GUESS WHAT HAPPENS. **YOU** DECIDE.

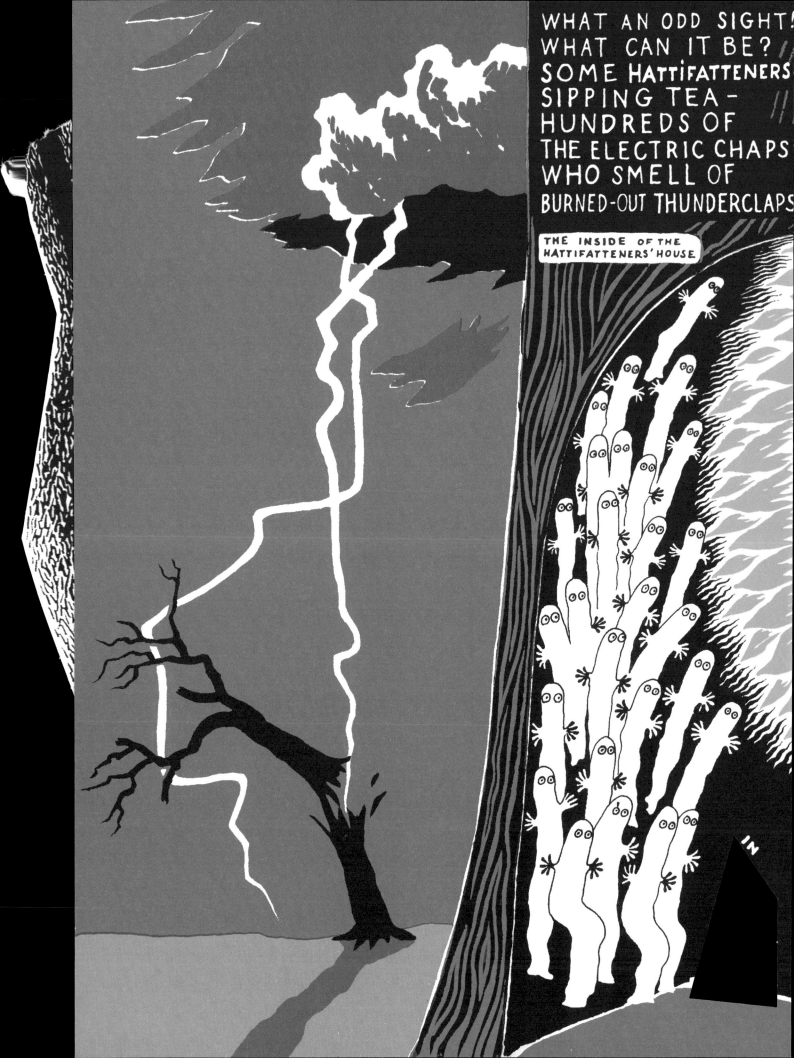

'Let's go,' said my...
We'd better dash
...efore they turn us
...nto ASH.'
...ATTERING HATS!'
...uffed *Mymble* 'QUICK!'
...OW GUESS WHAT
...APPENS IN A **TICK**.

OUT

Millions of sopping rain drops fall.
They get a soaking, one and all
Except for LITTLE MY, quite jolly
Underneath her lovely brolly).
The ground, already rather wet
From *Mymble's* tears, gets wetter yet.
MOOMINTROLL cries. 'We need dry land!'
Wait – here's someone to lend a hand:

On the horizon, two big ears
And, in between, the sun appears,
Our friends will soon be found, not lost.
NOW GUESS WHAT HAPPENS. **FINGERS CROSSED**.

'Welcome home, MOOMIN, safe and sound,
And welcome, friends! Come, gather round!'
What a relief it is to tell
A tale that ends supremely well,
Where lovely *Moominmamma* sat
Collecting BERRIES in a hat.
'Time for a feast,' said *Mamma*. 'Drink!'
Scrumptious delights all round, I think.
A shell, a rose, a fresh baked bun?
Oh, I'm so glad to see my son,
And gorgeous milk! There's milk galore!'
NOW GUESS WHAT HAPPENS, JUST ONCE MORE.

YUCK! All the milk's turned sour and cheesy.
Mamma says 'Never mind, it's easy:
Now we've all got a great excuse
For drinking SWEET PINK BERRY JUICE!'

THIS HOLE –
–The very last you see –
They can't get through–it's much too wee.
'We'll stay here in this book, and why?
'CAUSE WE'RE TOO BIG !!!' said LITTLE MY.